Little Red Rolls Away

By Linda Whalen and Illustrated by Jennifer E. Morris

PUBLISHED BY SLEEPING BEAR PRESS

The little red barn creaked awake.
He listened for Rooster's crow,
Piglet's squeal, and Bossy Cow's moo.

But all was quiet.
Where were his friends?
Everything was missing.

No hay.
No grain.
No tools.

Red was empty.

Gears rumbled.
Engines hummed.
Metal monsters surrounded Red.

Giant jacks slid beneath Red.
His right side went up.
His left side went up.
He lifted right off of the ground.

A truck with long metal bars and big rugged wheels rolled under him.

Red dropped onto the bars.

Gears rumbled.
Slowly, Red moved down the lane.

He passed rows of corn, farmers in fields,
cows grazing, railroad tracks, and small towns.

He stopped at the bank of a big wide river.

TOOT! TOOT!

Two tugboats pushed a long barge to the pier.

Red did NOT like this trip one bit!

WHIZZ! CLACK!! CLANG!

Red looked up to see a big hook swinging over his roof.

Wide straps wrapped over, under, and all around him. The big hook scooped him up.

Red's boards shook.
His nails nearly popped out.

SWOOSH! CLACK! *CLANG!*

The hook swung him onto the barge.

Waves splashed.
The barge rocked.
A silver arch stretched across the sky.

When the barge stopped, another hook grabbed Red.
He was on the road again.

HONK! HONK!

People pointed. Children clapped.

The sounds faded as he left the city.
Clouds gathered.
The sky rumbled.
Red rolled into deep, dark woods.

Where was he going?
He missed Rooster, Piglet, and even Bossy Cow.
Would he ever see his friends again?

Another metal monster looped high above the trees.
Red locked his doors.
He closed his windows tight.

Red rolled out of the woods and into . . .

...an amusement park!!!!!

Again, giant jacks slid beneath Red.
His left side went up.
His right side went up.
Big rugged wheels rolled away.

PLOP!!

Red lowered to the ground.

POTTING SOIL
OATS

A farm truck roared up to his door.
Hay filled his loft. Grain spilled into his bin.
Tools were hung on his wall. But something was missing.
Until . . .

Rooster crowed, Piglet squealed,
and Bossy Cow mooed.
Red's friends were back!
And there were even new friends to get to know!

BANG! THUMP!

A sign rose over Red's door.

Red knew he would love his new home!

WELCOME TO THE
PETTING ZOO!
z Z z Z z z z Z z